Goodnight Lovebug

Written By: T.L.Clause

Illustrated By: Nina Gvozdeva

Dedication:

To the joy of reading.

This is a
Lovebug.

This Lovebug likes to snuggle and hug.

You can love this Lovebug in the morning.

You can love
this Lovebug
at noon.

You can love this Lovebug in the evening when the day is through.

When the day
is ended
and it is
time to
go to bed;
this Lovebug
will help you get cozy
and rest your
little head.

Your eyes feel heavy. Lovebug's eyes feel heavy. It is time to get ready for bed.

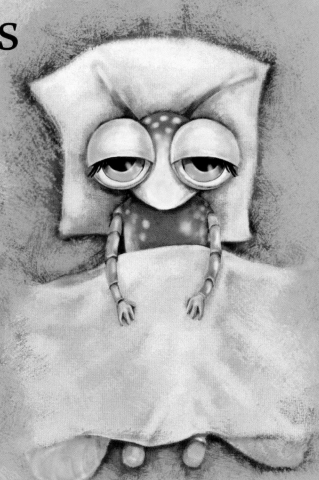

So, close
your eyes
and go to sleep.

The day has ended.

The
day is
complete.

And while you sleep,
know that you are loved.

Because you and
Lovebug
are very
special
indeed.

So, close your eyes and rest your sleepy head.

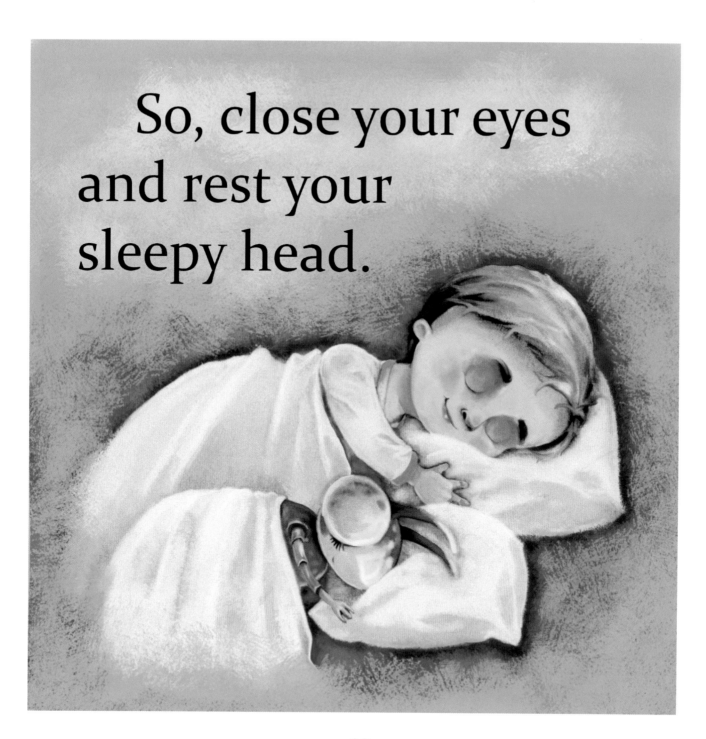

Close your eyes and go to sleep.

And while you sleep
have sweet dreams.

Your day is ended. Lovebug's day is ended. Your day is complete. Lovebug's day is complete.

You and Lovebug
are getting sleepy.

And while you sleep
know that you
are being
watched over
and will
always
be taken
very good
care of.

The sun has set.

The moon is shining.

The stars are
brightly shining
in the sky.

You and Lovebug are so very tired. Yawning, it is time for bed.

So, close your eyes and
dream with Lovebug.
Close your eyes
and go to sleep.

You and Lovebug
are tucked into bed.

You are
dreaming.
Lovebug is
dreaming.

25

Your eyes are closed.
Lovebug's eyes
are closed.

You are resting.
Lovebug is resting.

You are asleep.
Lovebug is asleep.

Goodnight to you.
Goodnight
to Lovebug.

Sweet dreams to you. Sweet dreams to Lovebug.

Goodnight.

I will see you
and Lovebug in the
morning when
you both wake.

The end.

33

Until Tomorrow ......

Made in the USA
Columbia, SC
27 November 2019